The Uncuddibles

The Fright Before Christmas

Written and illustrated by
RJ Thompson

The Uncuddibles

The Fright Before Christmas

Written and illustrated by
RJ Thompson

One cold and snowy Christmas Eve.
The Uncuddibles sat together around their Christmas tree.
PJ's on and their stockings hanging ready.
Roasting marshmallows and stuffing their fluffy bellies.

"I'm too excited" said Shadow whilst eating her sweets.
"Well you won't get any presents if you don't just go to sleep"
chuckled Bulk.

Then just as The Uncuddibles started to settle down.
Screech!, Smash! and Wallop!, "What was that awful sound?"
said Creepy.
"I'm not quite sure, but we better go and see.
The last time I recall, it was that crazy little B3" said Bony.

The Uncuddibles could see something stuck on the roof.
It was black, white and red but it had boots and some hoofs.

The bears climbed the stairs and emerged at the top.

They pulled on the boots and out Santa popped!

The Uncuddibles were excited but very sad to see.
That poor old Santa had clearly hurt his knee.
"Ho Ho Owwww!" said Santa in pain.

Santa tried to get up, but he fell over again!

Santa explained that whilst flying high above.
His sleigh was hit was a massive green blob.
"I have no idea where it came from" he said.
"I bet I can guess" said Bulk turning red.

Yes, those naughty green mice had been using their catapult. "If you've ruined Christmas, this will all be your fault!" shouted Dash.

"I'm afraid this may come as a bit of a fright..
But I will need you to deliver all the presents tonight."
said Santa

"Rudolph feels sick, I've hurt my knee and my head,
You will all have to help out and pretend to be Santa instead.

"The only problem is, my sleigh is broken you see?"
"That's ok Santa, we'll just call The Hay Team"
said Clark.

The Hay Team helped out and built a fizz-popping sleigh.
They packed up the presents and then went on their way.

"The children want Santa, not a sleigh full of bears.
We'll have to dress up so that no kids are scared." said Bulk.

Bulk found some Christmas costumes in the factory toy box.
There was Santa, Rudolph, an elf and a fox.

"Some cotton wool for a snowman" said Dee.
"I'll be the Grinch and Creepy can be a tree!"

"Wow! you guys look great, although I must insist.
Don't go on your adventure without my naughty list"
said Santa

Dash scanned the list with his robotic eye.
While The Uncuddibles got ready to take to the sky.

As The Uncuddibles got ready to leave.
The naughty green mice snuck on board without being seen.
Shadow stood up, "Are we ready to go?"
"Three, two, one!" they shot off through the snow!

First stop was New York and wow what a sight.
The City was glowing with bright coloured lights.

They packed up their sacks and shot off into the night.
Delivering presents and all sorts of delights.
While The Uncuddibles were gone from their sleigh.
The naughty green mice jumped out and ran away.

"New York is amazing, we'll have to come back" said Bony.
Then all of a sudden Clark felt a poke through his sack.

"Oh my, it's a little girl, where did you come from?
She must of climbed into the sleigh while we were gone."
said Bulk.

"Dent!" said the little girl as she pointed at Clark.
"How does she know my name?" he said as he looked
at his mark.

"I'm not quite sure but were running out of time,
She will have to come with us, keep her warm and she'll be fine."
smiled Bulk.

Clark wrapped the girl up and gave her a cuddle.
"We'll call you little 'A' until we sort out this muddle" he said.

Off up into the clouds and on to Japan.

Dash delivered the lot, running as fast as he can.

From London...

To Paris...

Then Africa...

To Rome...
The Uncuddibles made sure they got to everyone's home.

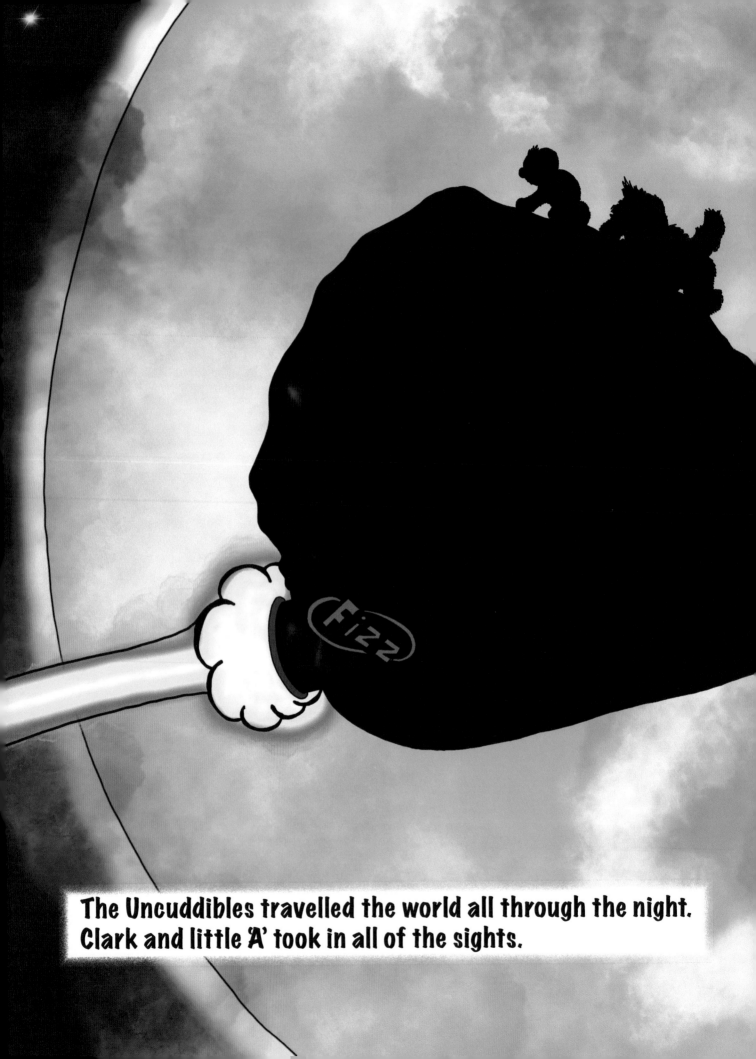

The Uncuddibles travelled the world all through the night.
Clark and little 'A' took in all of the sights.

"I think we're all done, let's get little 'A' back before the morning"
said Creepy.
"Yes we better hurry as she's just started yawning"
said Clark.

"How will we know where she came from? asked Dee.
"We must keep our eyes open for any clues we might see"
said Clark

"Daddy!" said little 'A' as she saw the big 'A.'
The Uncuddibles came to a stop and got out of their sleigh.

The Uncuddibles found an open window where 'A' had clearly got out.
"Bye bye" screamed 'A', "Sssh little one, whisper don't shout" said Bulk

Little 'A' hugged each Uncuddible and whispered good bye.
She turned around to Clark but to her surprise.

Clark was at the next window standing up on the shelf.
Clark turned and looked sadly towards everyone else.

For inside the window Clark saw a boy.
Asleep holding a poster about a missing toy.

A tear trickled down as Clark sighed with a groan. "That's why she knows my name... this was my home.."

Little 'A' tugged at Clark's paw and tried to pull him inside.
The Uncuddibles looked upset and Dee started to cry.

Clark turned around and knew what he had to do.
"We understand Clark, this is the right place for you" said Shadow.

The Uncuddibles waved goodbye and launched into the night.
Little 'A' ran into her brothers room and switched on the light.

"Dent! Dent!" she shouted as the boy rose from his bed.
Little 'A' yanked his hand and pulled him out to the roof ledge.

Meanwhile The Uncuddibles arrived back at the toy factory to find.
Santa and Rudolph having a whale of a time.

"Hang on a minute" said Dash, "I thought you hurt your knee?"
"Well" said Santa, "We had some of this lovely cake and it seems to have fixed me!".

The Uncuddibles laughed and Dash yelled "Let's get this party started!"
They all tried to have fun but still felt heavy hearted.

For The Uncuddibles missed their little blue bear...
"I hope Clark's ok and having fun somewhere out there" sobbed Dee.

"It's freezing out here April, have you forgotten?" smiled the boy.

"Dent" sighed April as she picked up the pile of cotton.
The boy had a look, picked her up and then said.
"Come on little one, let's get you back in to bed".

April and the boy turned around quick.
For there on the cotton wool sat a nicely wrapped gift.

Back at the factory, the bears looked out across the falling snow.
Then to their surprise Shadow noticed a red glow.

"What's that" she said as they all looked to the sky.
A familiar shadow cast over them, "Happy Christmas guys!"...

Christmas complete, all The Uncuddibles were back together.
Christmas cake all round in the glorious snowy weather.

Back in New York, April and her brother unwrapped their gift. It was a brand new camera with a special message within it.

They turned on the camera and both looked in surprise.
For there was Clark Dent, right before their eyes....

The Uncuddibles

The Uncuddibles Series - Available now at Amazon & on Kindle.

Follow us on facebook/Twitter and Instagram @theuncuddibles and you can also enjoy a full video read through of 'Book One' by Michelle Mead.

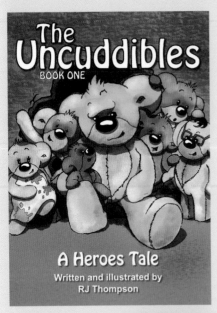

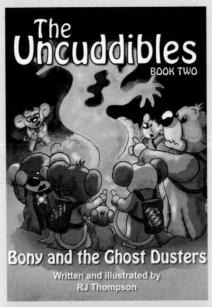

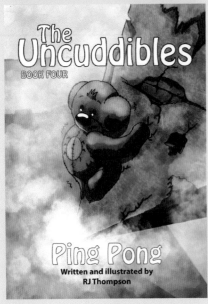

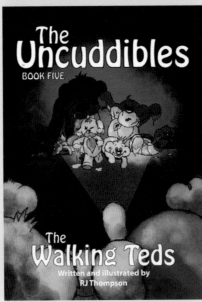

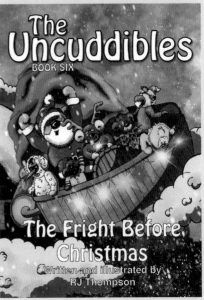

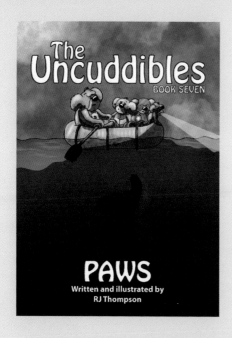
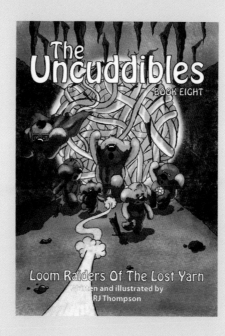
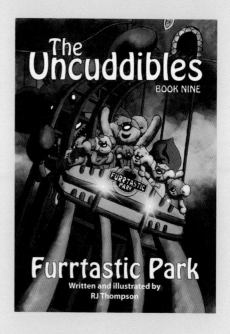

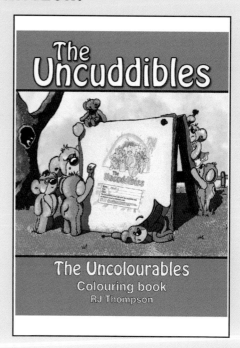

Printed in Poland
by Amazon Fulfillment
Poland Sp. z o.o., Wrocław